This book belongs to:

_____

_____

_____

_____

_____

Apple Pie Publishing

Apple Pie Publishing, LLC
P.O. Box 1135
Rockwall, TX 75087
www.applepiepub.com

Editors Judith Shapley and Kathleen Feigen
Book Design by Michael Albee - michaelalbee.com
Author Photo by J. Mathew Butler - jmathewinc.com

The text for this book is set in Optima, Century Gothic, and Candy Script. The illustrations in this book are rendered in colored pencil. Manufactured in the U.S.A. with lead free ink and paper.
10 9 8 7 6 5 4 3

Shapley-Box, Diane.
Fred Visits the Emerald Coast / written and illustrated
by Diane Shapley-Box.
-- 1st ed. p. cm.

SUMMARY: Fred, the frog, and his friends go on a vacation that turns out to be an exciting adventure. Fred makes interesting new friends from the amazing Emerald Coast.

Audience: Ages 2-8.
LCCN 2011916078
ISBN-13: 9780615536187

To my husband Kevin, sons Patrick and Mitchell

and to Mom and Dad

Apple Pie Publishing
Rockwall, TX

Fred Visits the Emerald Coast

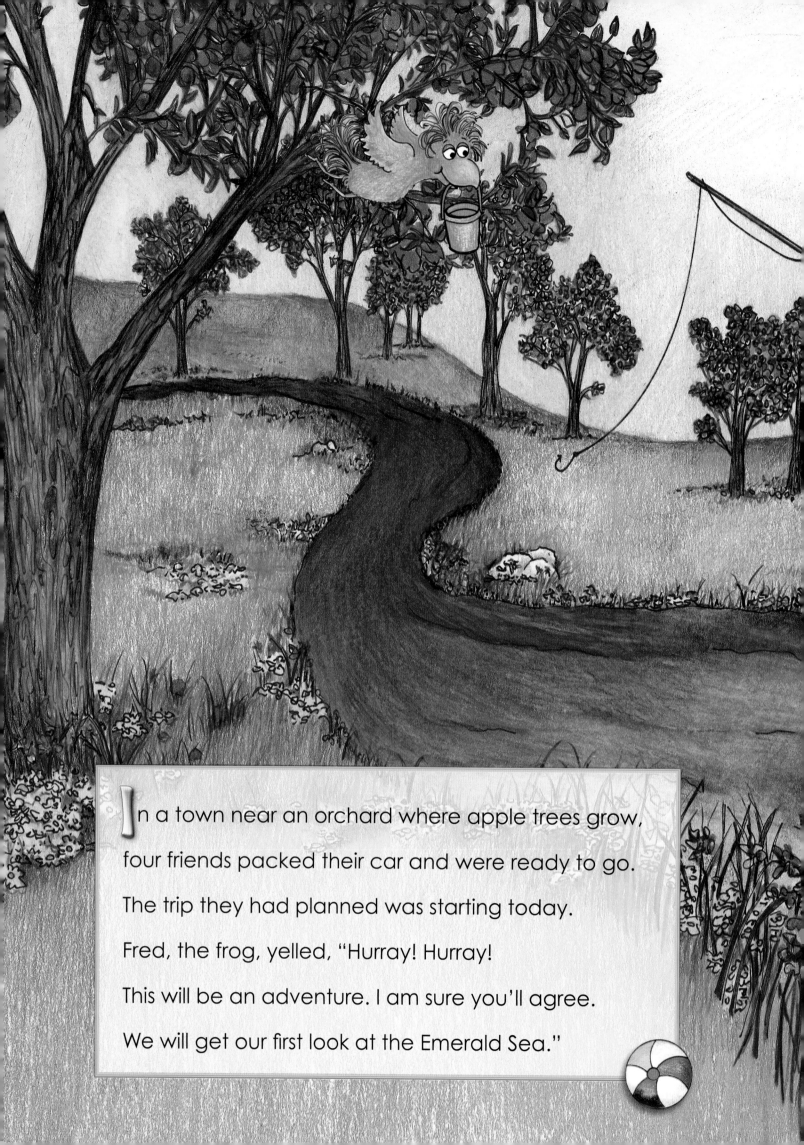

In a town near an orchard where apple trees grow,

four friends packed their car and were ready to go.

The trip they had planned was starting today.

Fred, the frog, yelled, "Hurray! Hurray!

This will be an adventure. I am sure you'll agree.

We will get our first look at the Emerald Sea."

The friends drove all day and the next day too.

Then Fred spotted water that was greenish blue.

The ground sparkled like new fallen snow,

with sand so white that it seemed to glow.

Fred said to his friends, "We are at the seashore!

I think I will go for a hop and explore."

Fred hopped up the beach. He hopped very far.

In the sand, he saw the shape of a star.

The star coughed and gasped then let out a wheeze.

He looked up at Fred and said, "Help me please."

"Sad little starfish, what do you need?" asked Fred.

"I got stuck in the sand," the sad starfish said.

"I need the ocean to breathe. The sea is my home.

I have been here all day scared and alone!"

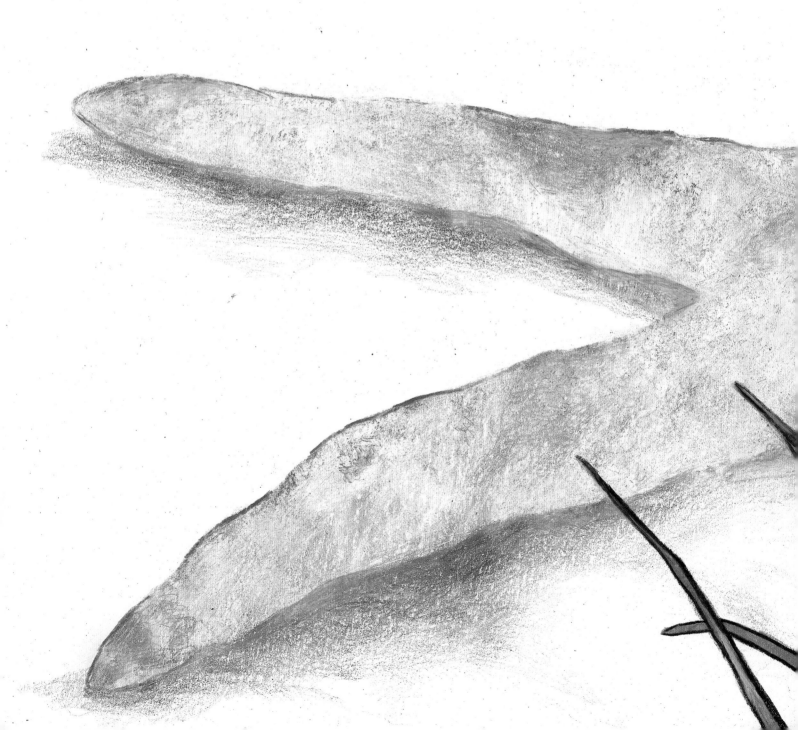

Fred scooped up the starfish and placed him in the sea.

The starfish wiggled and giggled then yelled, "I'm free!

No matter if you live near or far,

I will be your friend wherever you are."

The sky had been blue, but now it was black.

Fred knew it was late so he headed back.

He hopped down the beach at a very fast pace,

where he met a sea turtle with tears on her face.

"Sea turtle, why are you crying?" asked Fred.

She pointed to the tiki torches and said,

"My babies are headed where they should not be,

drawn toward the fire's light instead of the sea."

"I know what I can do!" Fred let out a shout.

He poured sand on the flames, and the fires went out.

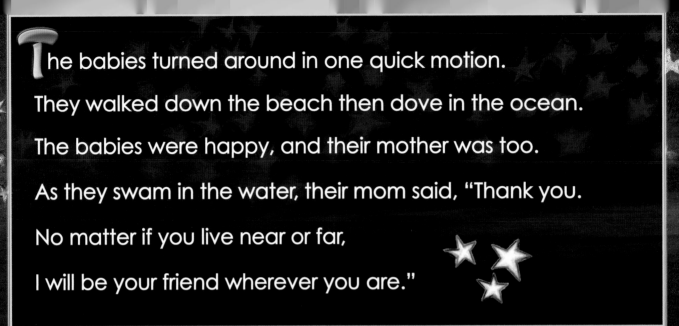

The babies turned around in one quick motion.

They walked down the beach then dove in the ocean.

The babies were happy, and their mother was too.

As they swam in the water, their mom said, "Thank you.

No matter if you live near or far,

I will be your friend wherever you are."

The next day Fred and his old pals went sailing.

Fred climbed on a sea chest next to the railing.

A huge wave crashed against the side of the ship.

Fred flew through the air and did a back flip.

Frightened and frazzled he began to yell.

In the sinking sea chest Fred, the frog, fell.

The lid closed tight as Fred sank in the sea.
Fred was locked inside, and there was no key!

The sea turtle and starfish heard Fred's cry.

They wanted to help and were determined to try.

The sea turtle swam swiftly toward Fred.

She lifted the sea chest over her head.

Through the water she paddled up to the boat.

With the chest on her shell, she started to float.

Clinging to the lock was Fred's starfish friend.

He stared at the lock, and then he started to bend.

His body formed into the shape of a key.

His arms slid into the lock and set Fred free.

Fred hopped on the boat and yelled, "Woo-eee!

Thank you so much for saving me.

No matter if you live near or far,

I will be your friend wherever you are."

Fred traveled back home and unpacked his suitcase.

Memories of his trip put a smile on his face.

Fred's adventure was fun at the Emerald Coast,

but the friendships he made were what mattered the most.

Fun Facts

Female sea turtles lay their eggs on the sand at the seashore. After they hatch, the babies must find their way to the sea. They should be drawn to the moon's reflection on the water. However, the bright lights on beach houses and streets can confuse the turtles and cause them to go the wrong way.

A sea horse will use its tail to hold on to sea grass so it can stay in one place.

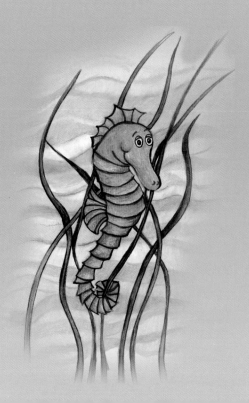

If a starfish loses an arm, it will grow back.

Crab's eyes can look forward, backward and side~to~side.

An octopus changes colors to fit in with their surroundings.

Dolphins are social animals and tend to live in families and groups.

Emerald Coast

Diane Shapley-Box
Author & Illustrator

Diane Shapley-Box started her career as a concept designer but soon realized her passion was to write and illustrate stories for young children.

The Apple Bunch Books series has won numerous awards nationally and internationally. Diane is inspired by her love of art, animals, and personal experiences. She credits much of her success to helpful family members.

Diane explains, " I am fortunate to have lived in many places across the country and believe this has helped me create the Apple Bunch Books series. My goal is to tell a story children will enjoy, while teaching them about different places in the United States. All of my books include important lessons and show the Apple Bunch buddies being kind and helpful."

Learn more about Diane and her books at
www.applepiepub.com.

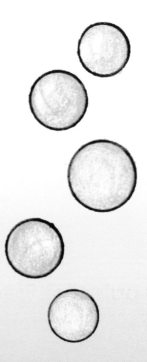

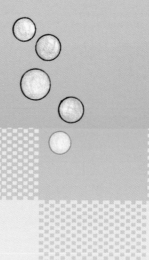

Collect all the
Apple Bunch
Books

QUALITY BOOKS MADE IN AMERICA

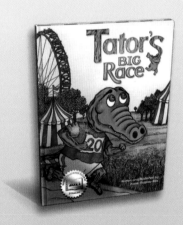
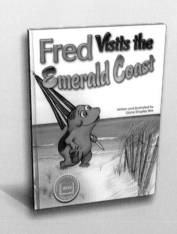